W9-BAF-667

Usborne

100 Paper Dragons

to Fold & Fly

Illustrated by Andy Elkerton

Designed by Hannah Ahmed and Brian Voakes

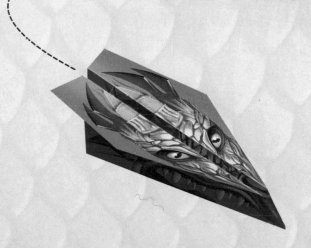

Turn over for tips on folding, flying and looking after your paper dragons.

Useful tips

Here are some helpful tips that will make your dragons fly more effectively and keep them in good condition.

How to launch your paper dragon

Here are the best steps to a perfect take-off and landing:

- Stand facing forward.

- Hold each dragon just in front of the middle of its body.

- Pull back and then throw forward in a long, smooth movement to release your dragon.

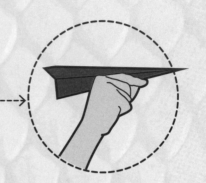

Folding

- Use a ruler to line up the folds and keep them sharp.

- If you want to keep your dragon for another day, store it flat inside a book.

- If your dragon gets wet, or won't fly... fold a new one!

Flying

- Try changing the angle of your dragon's wings to alter its flight.

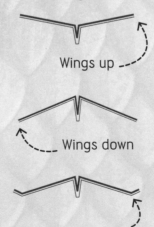

Wings up

Wings down

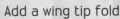

Add a wing tip fold

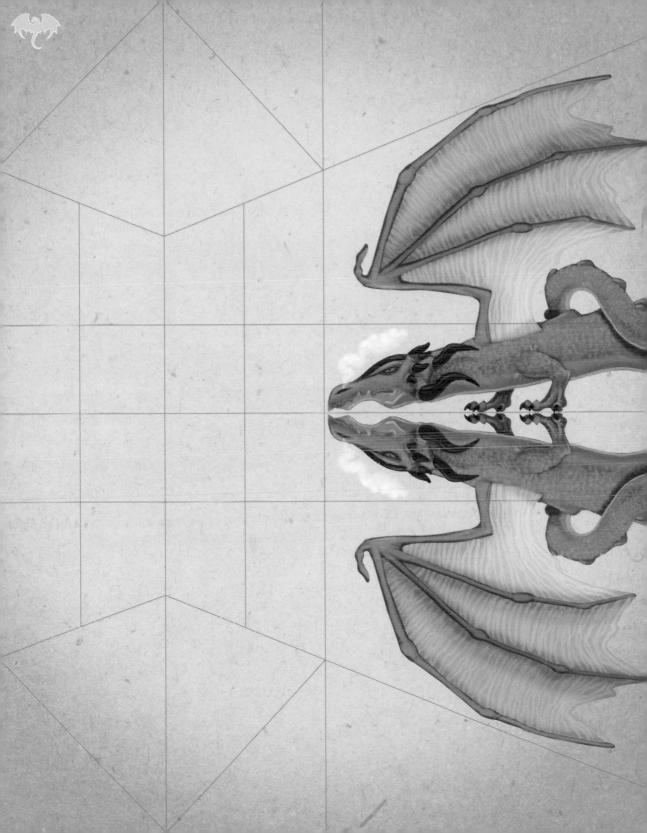

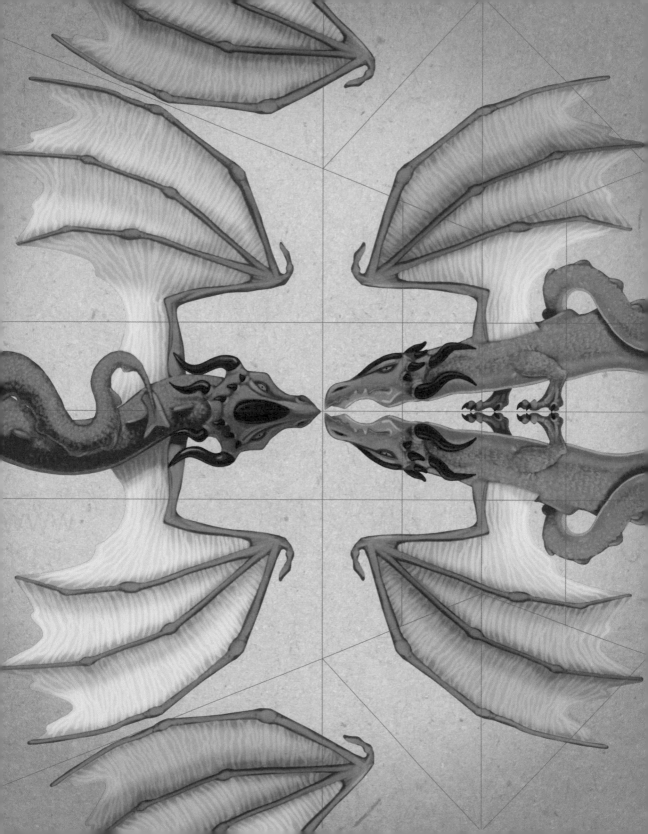

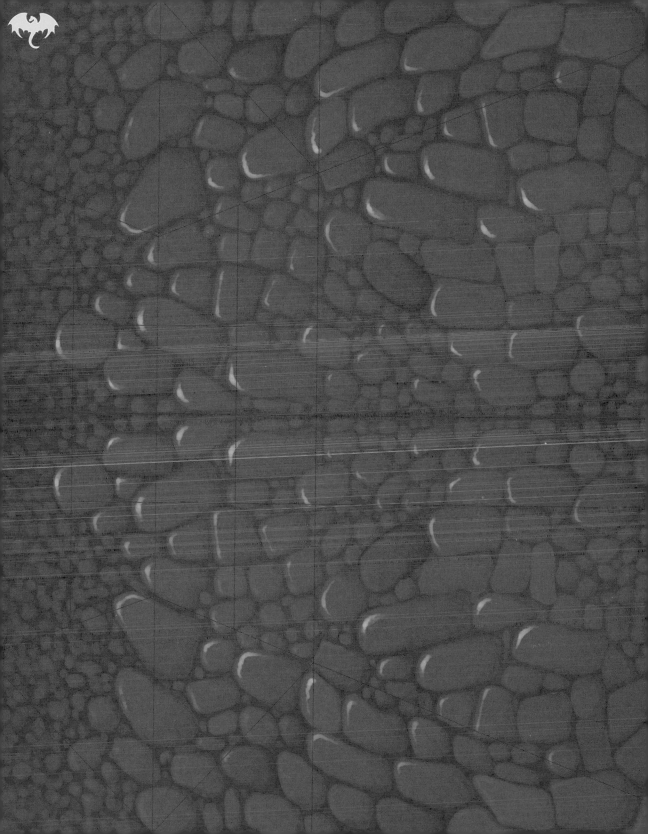

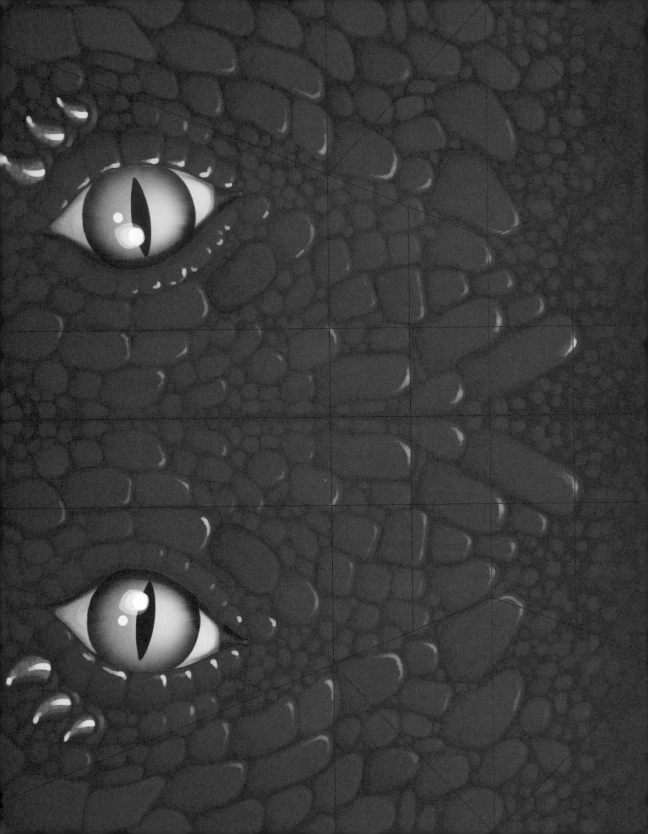

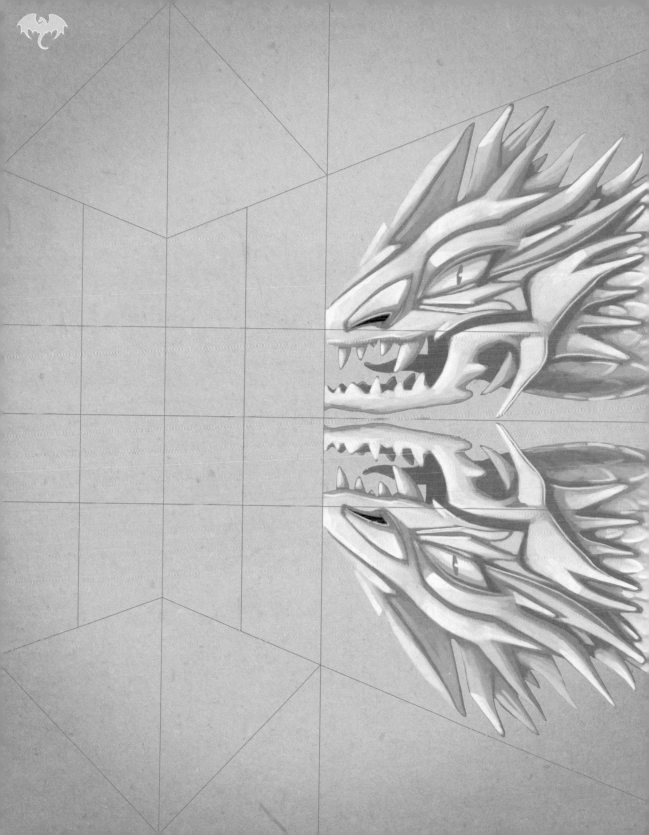

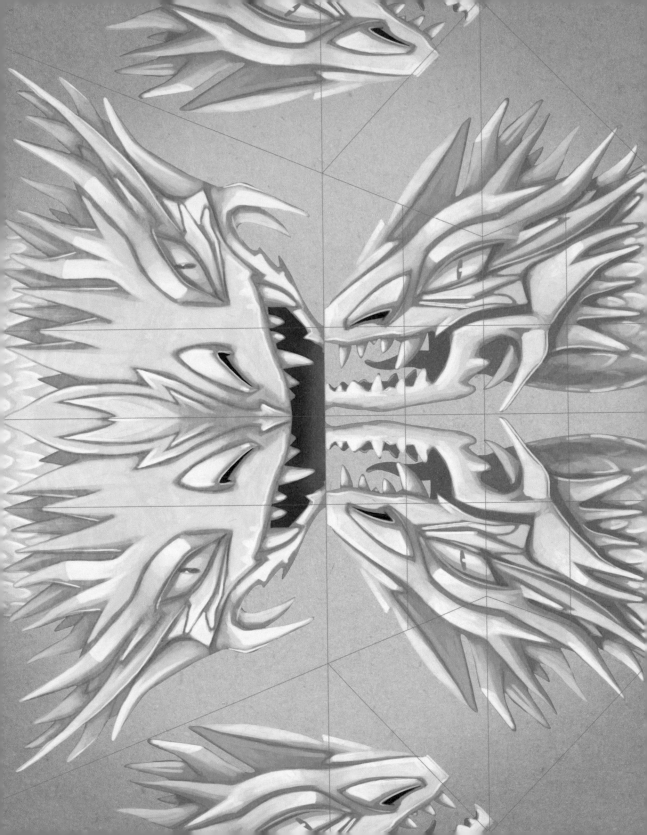

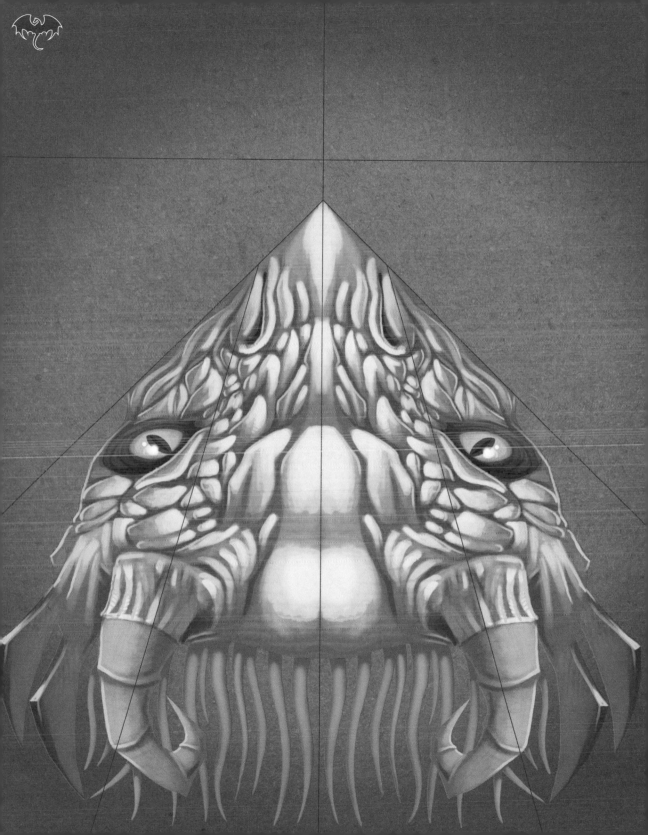

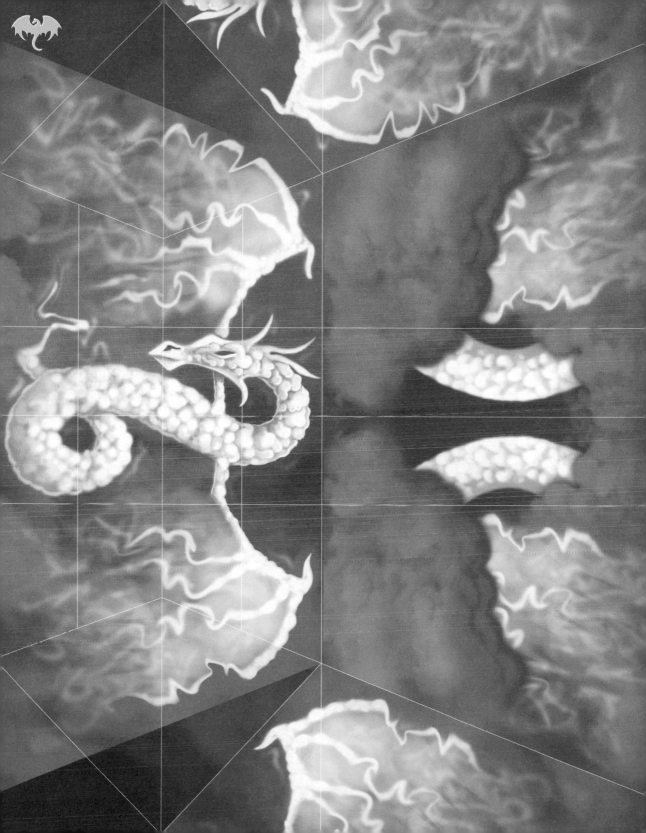

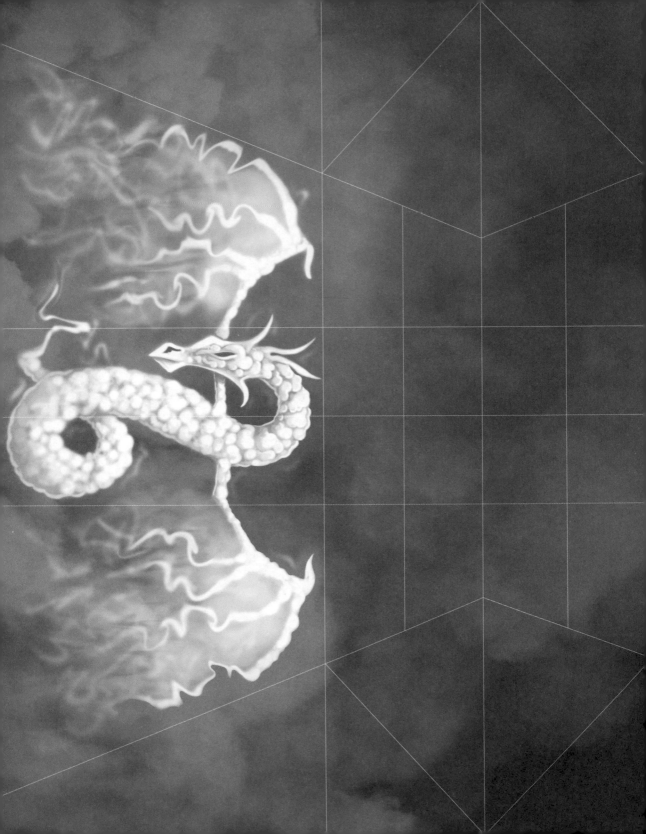

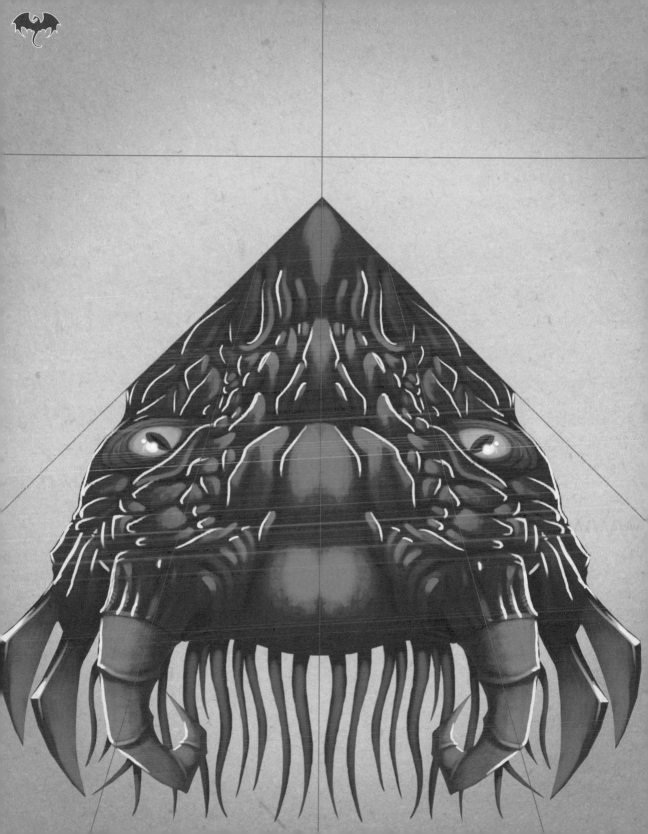

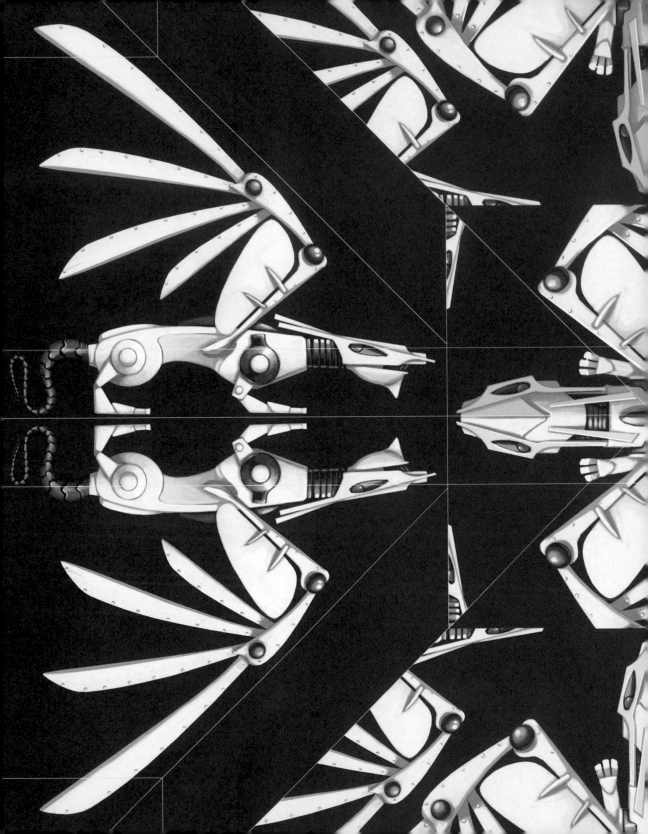

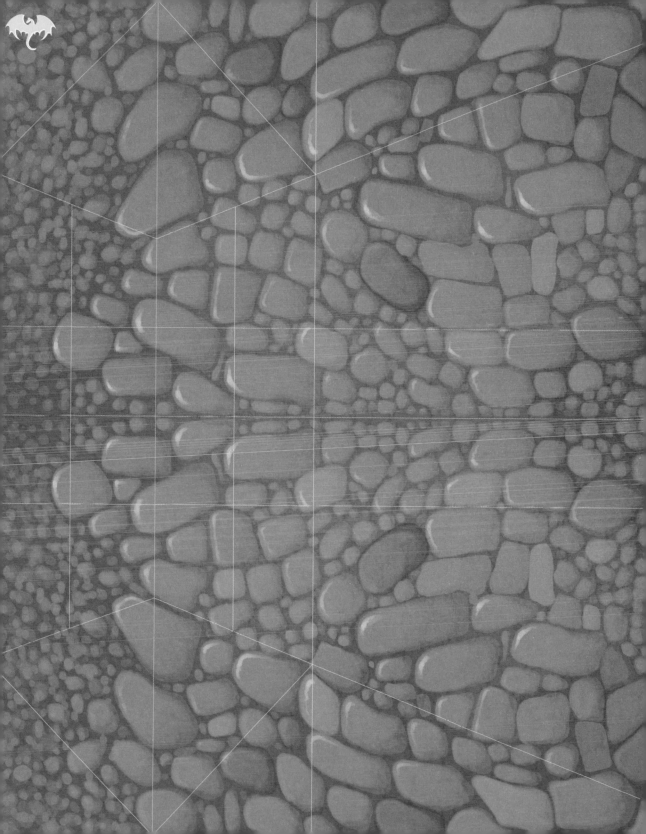

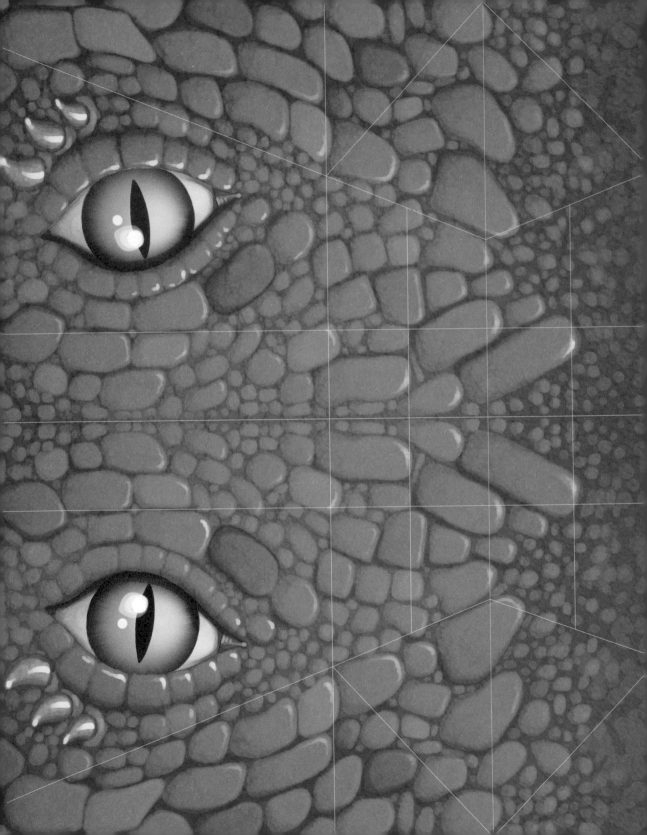

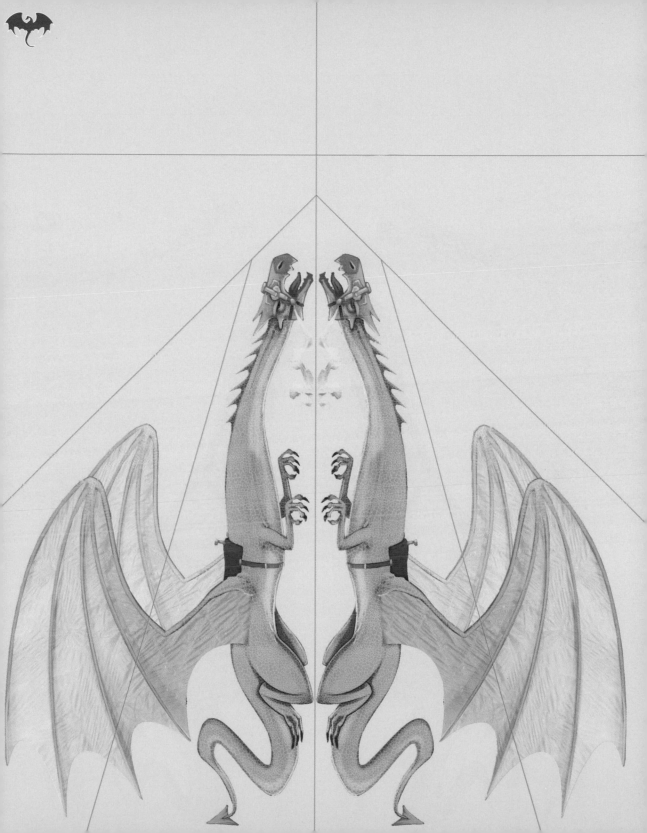

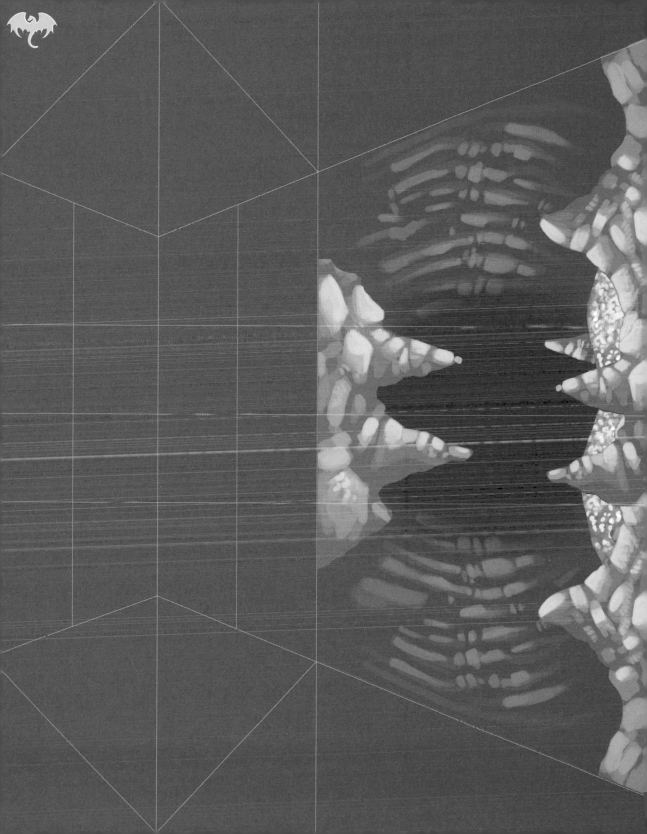

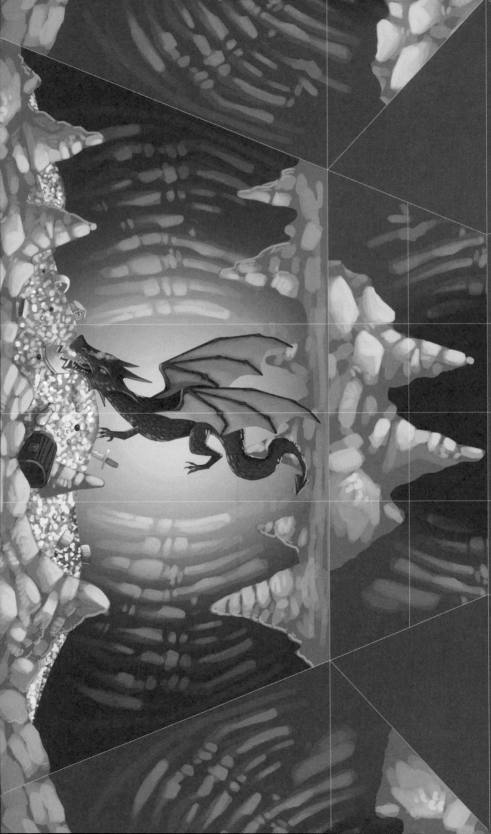

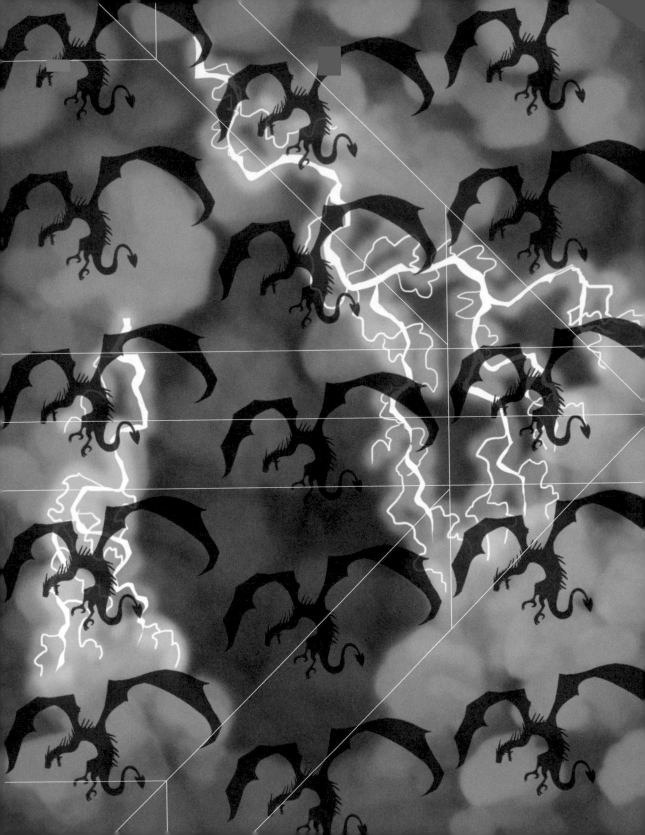

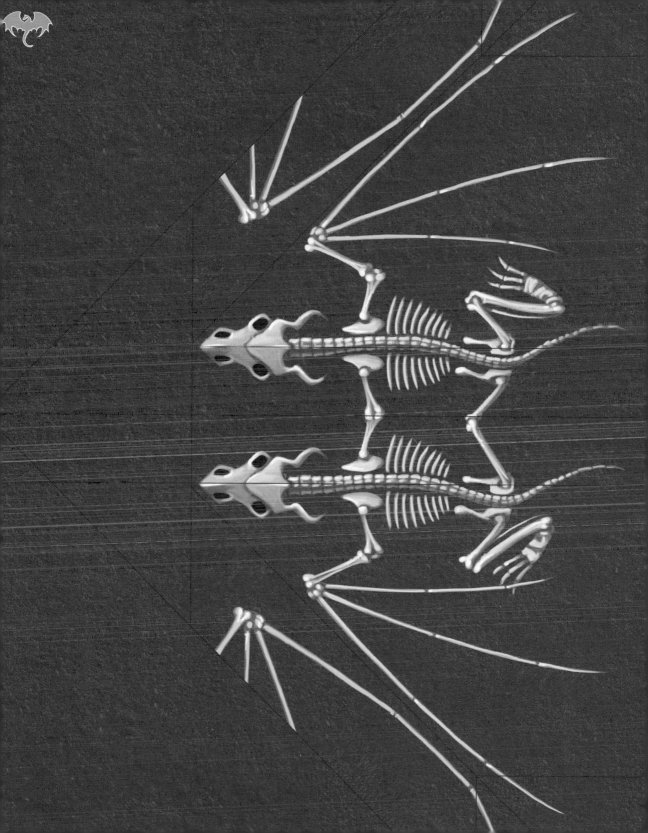

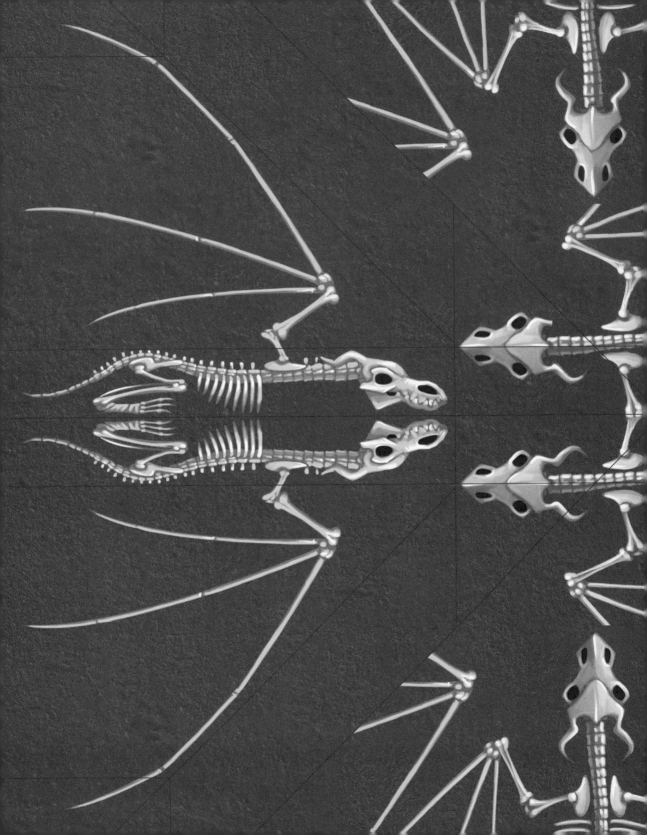

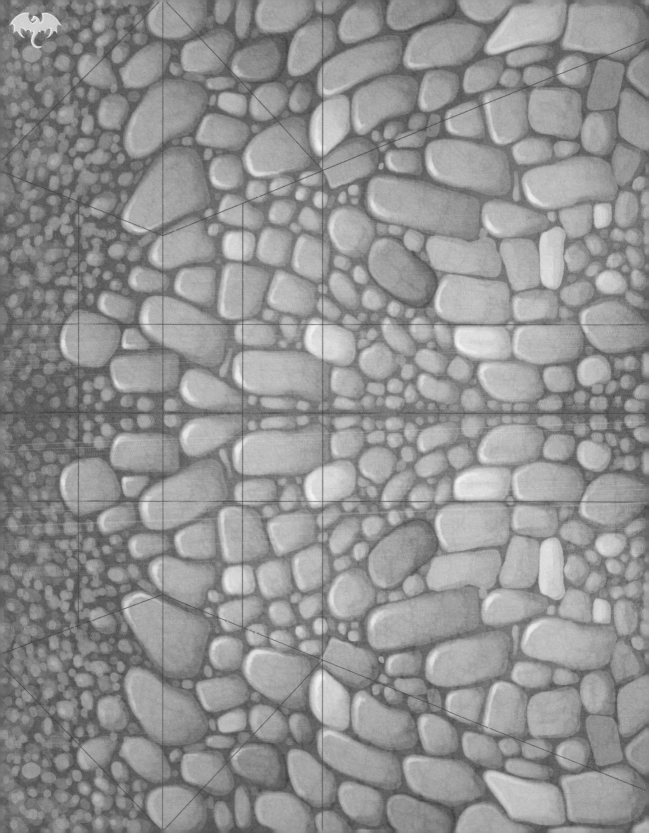

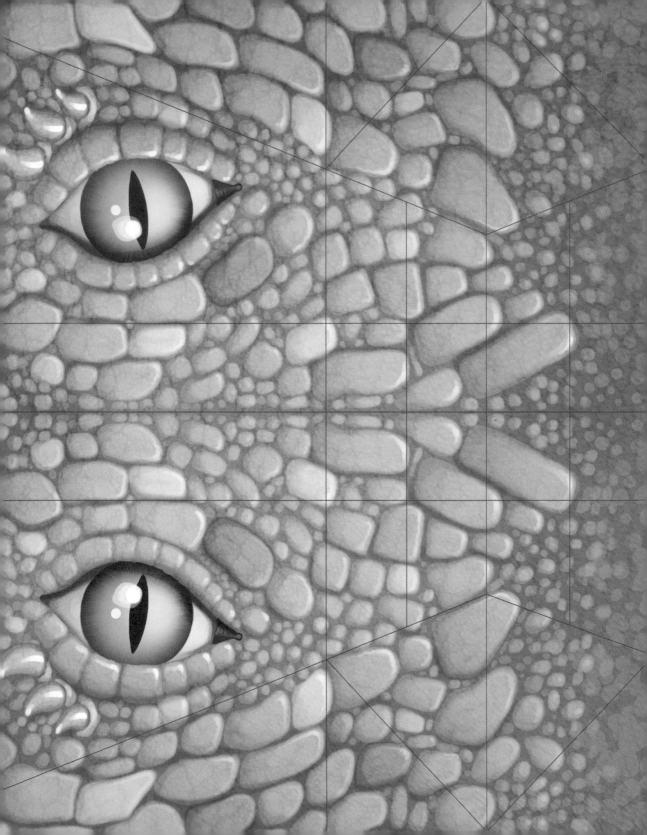

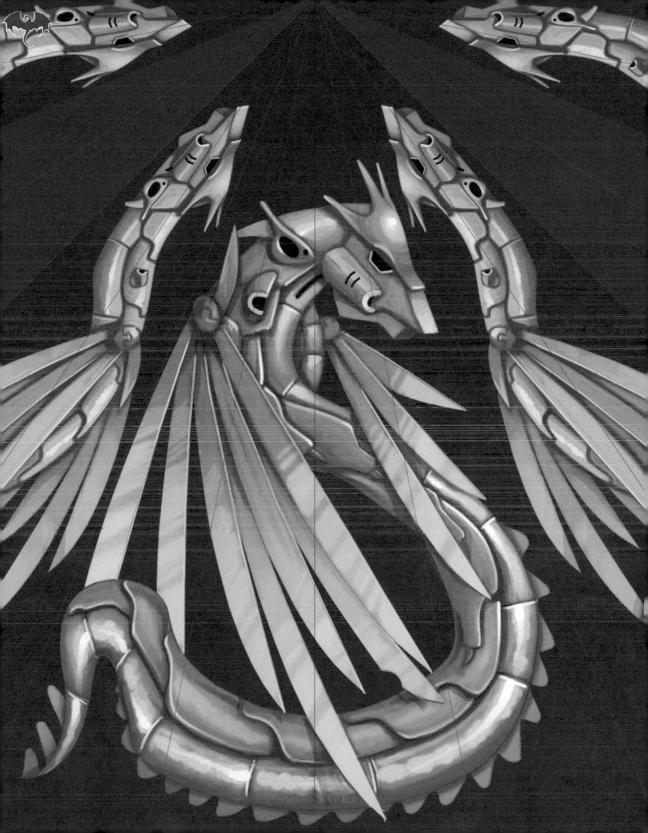

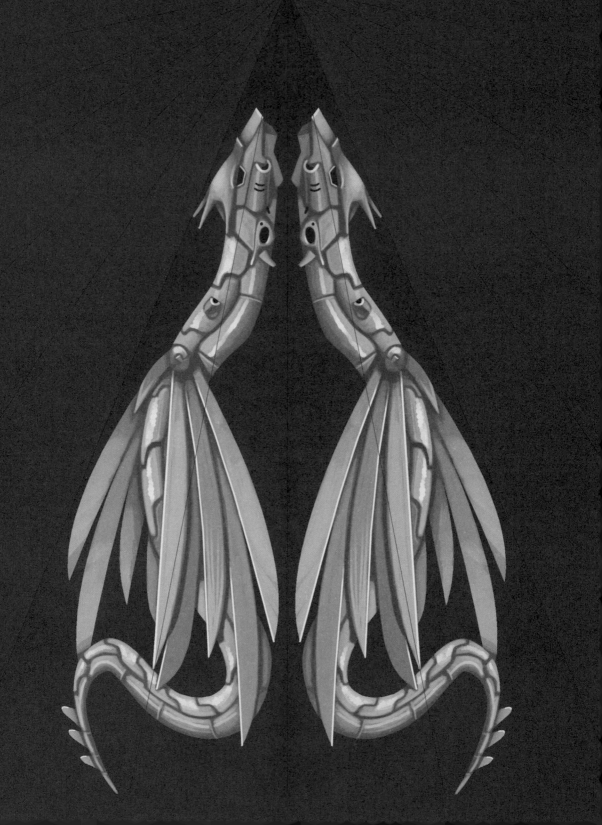

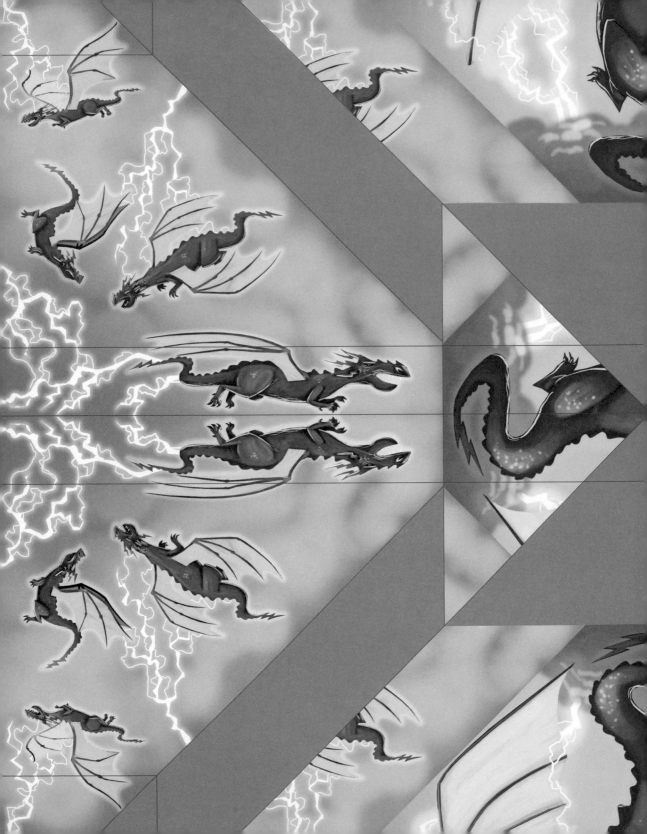

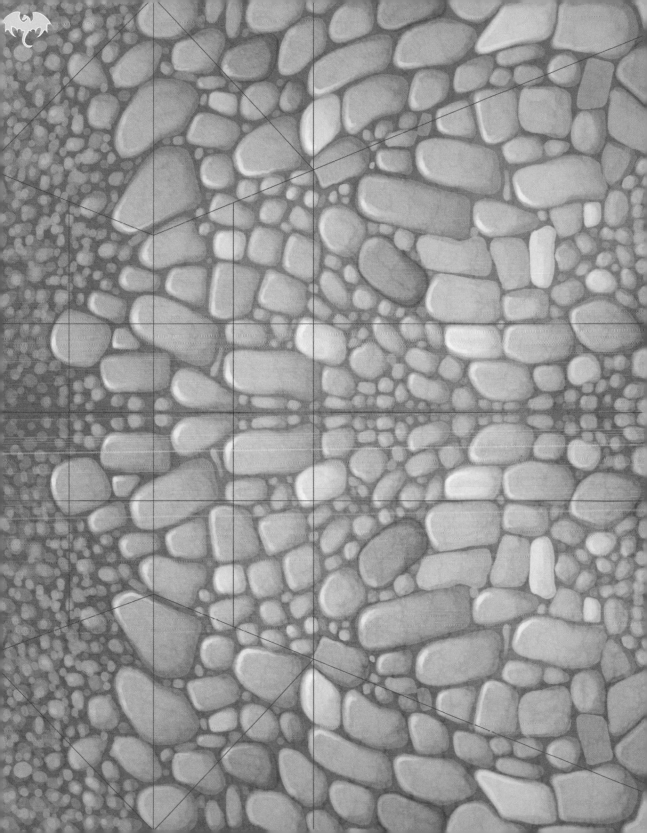

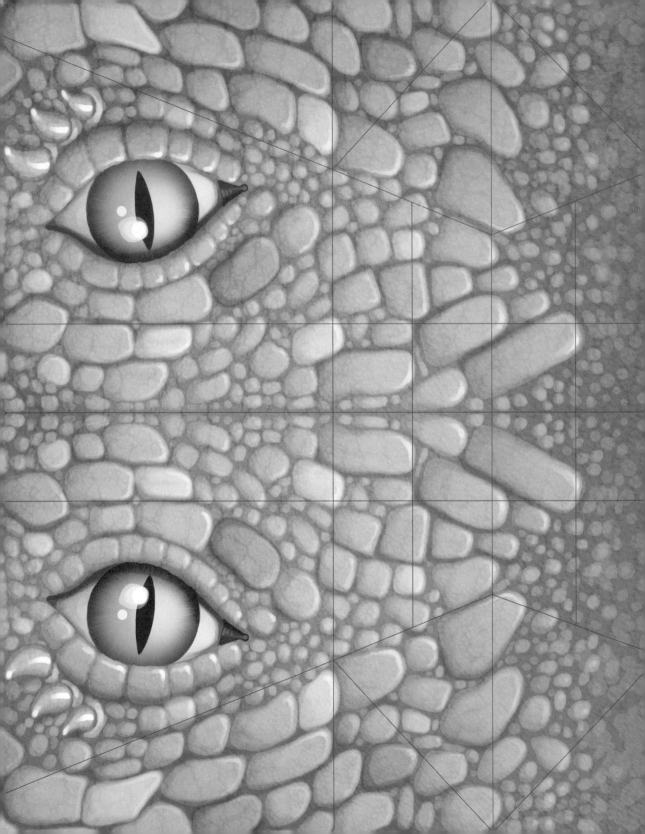

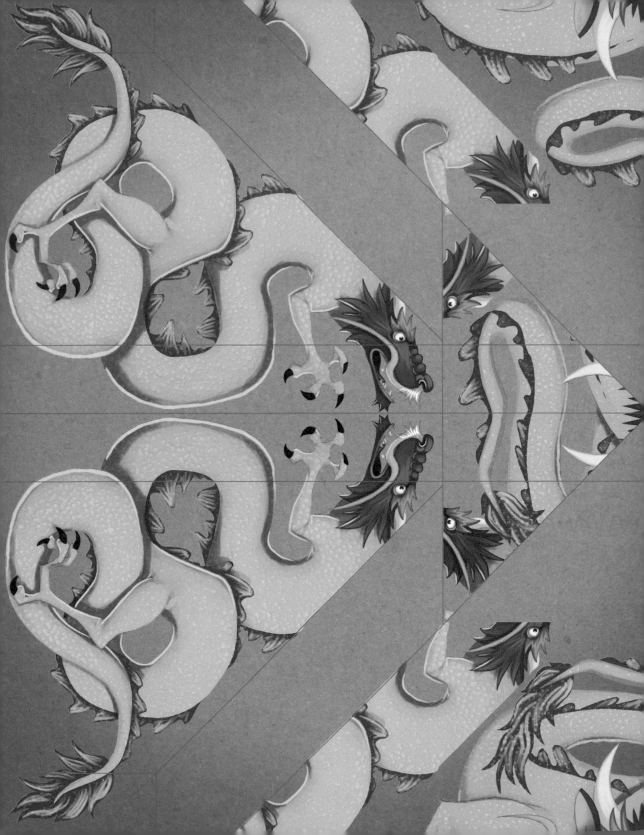

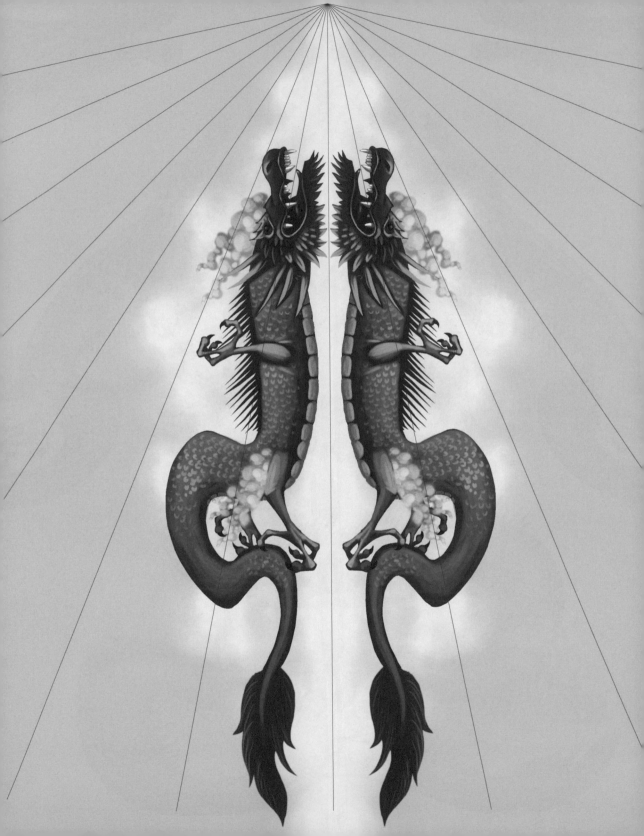

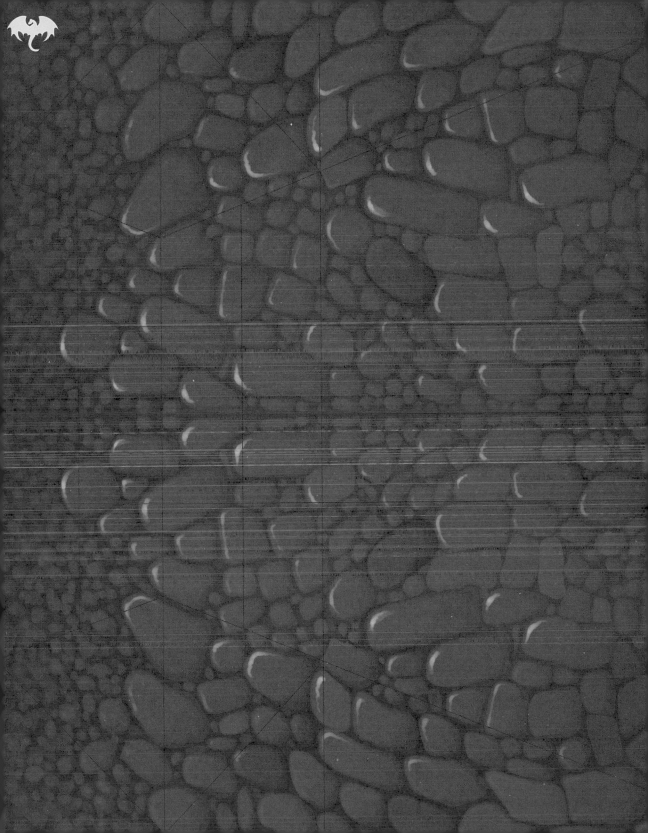

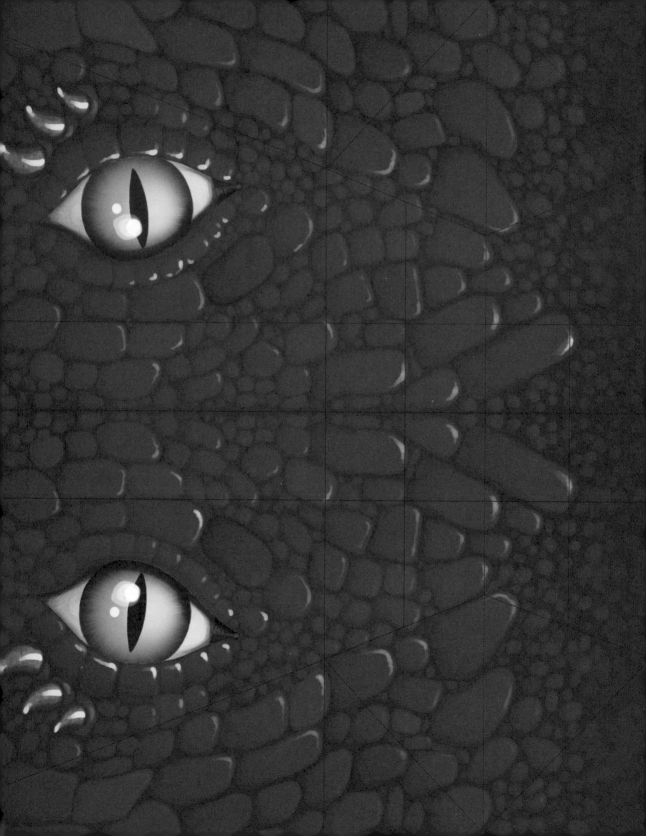

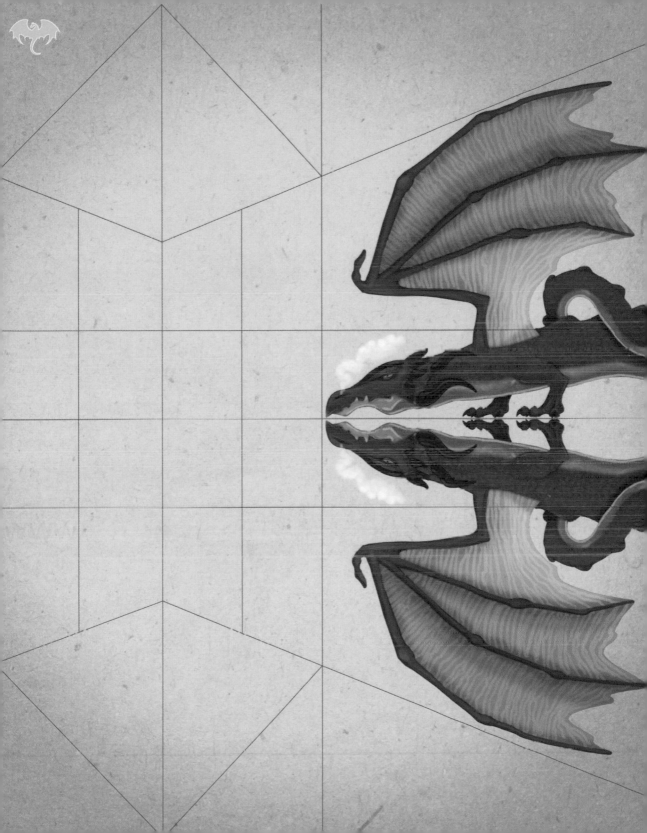

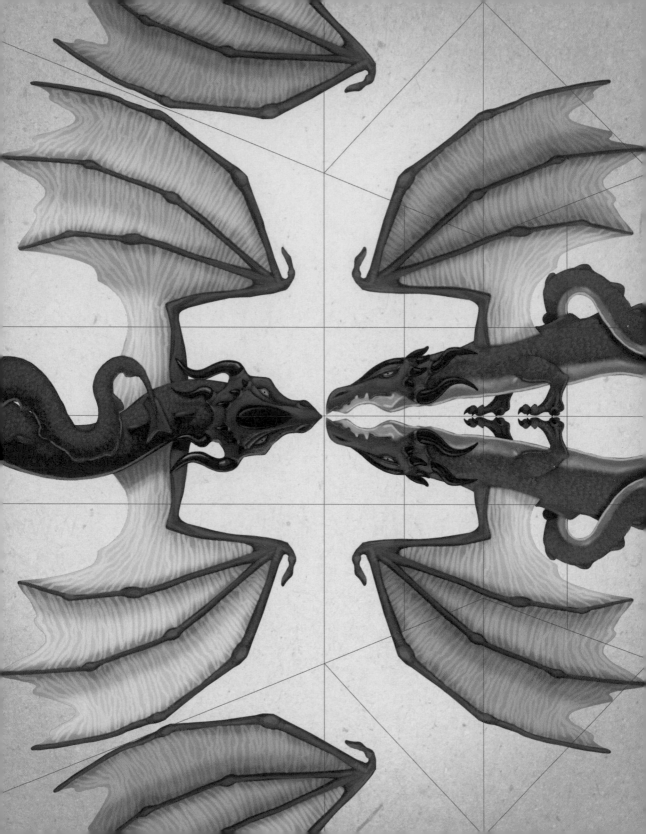

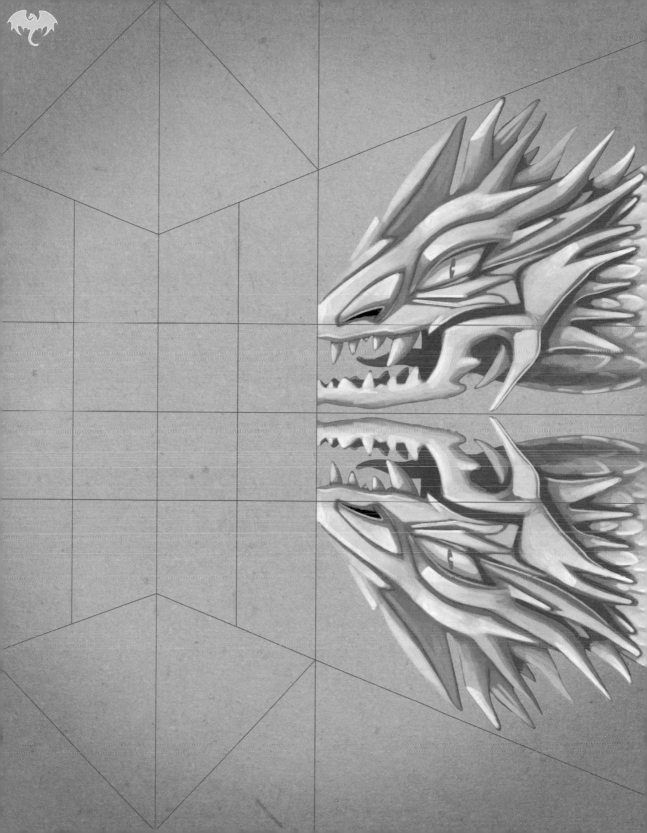

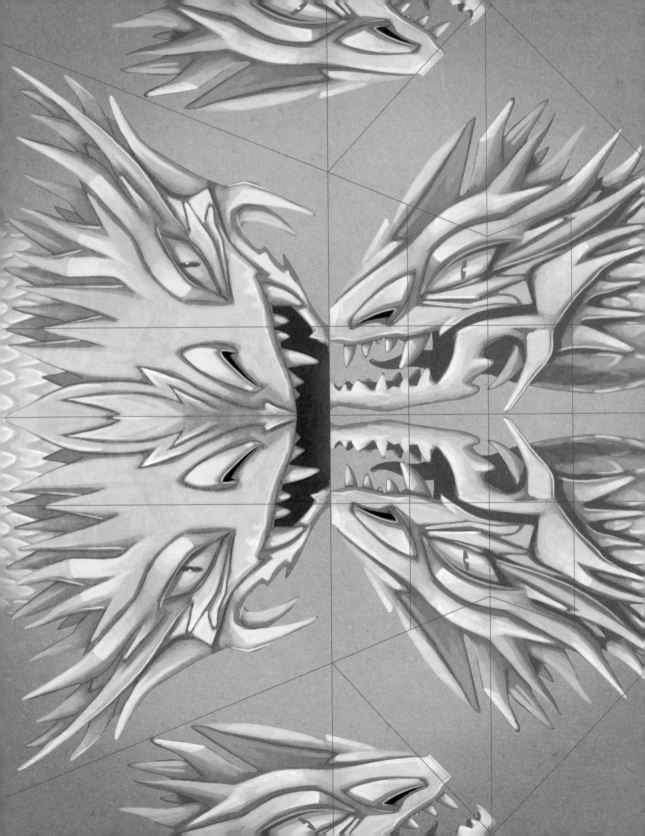

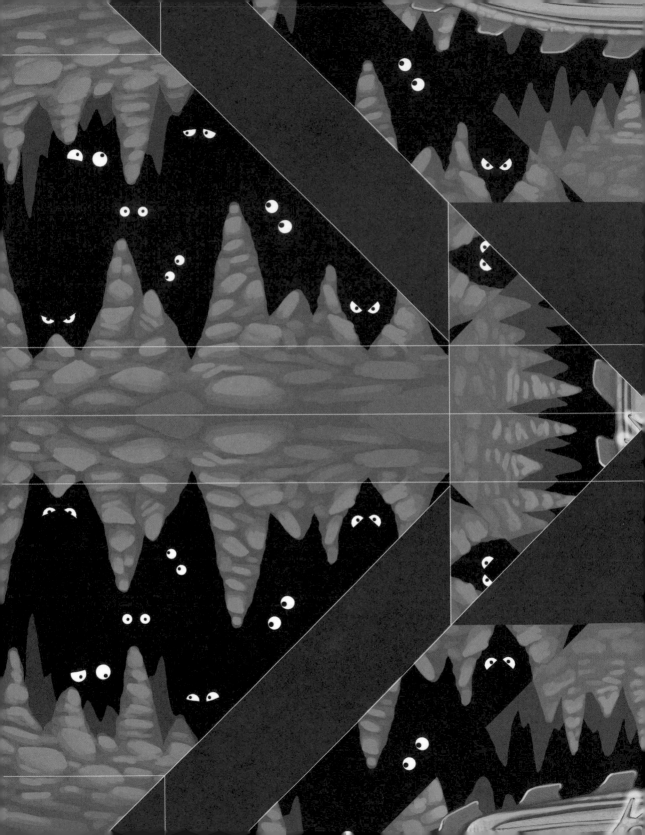

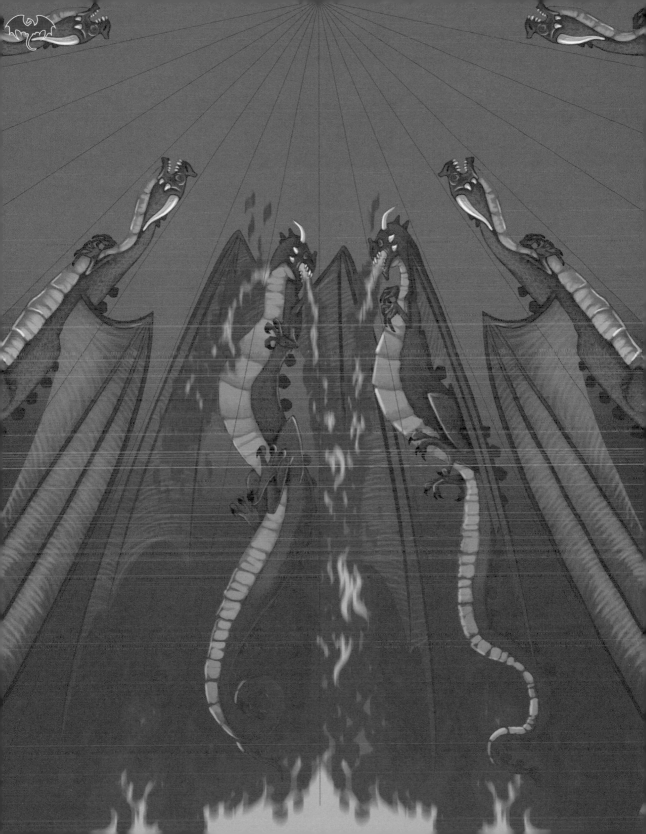

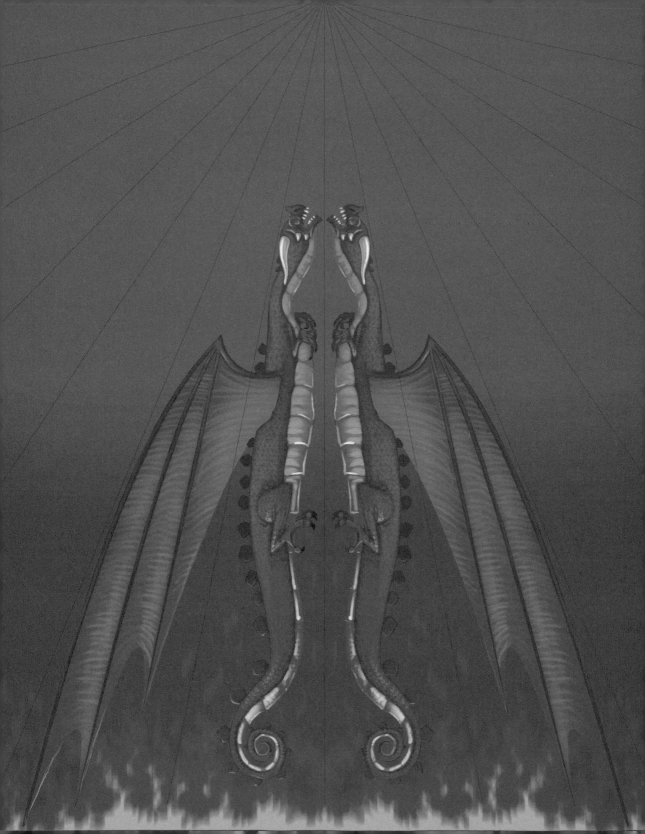

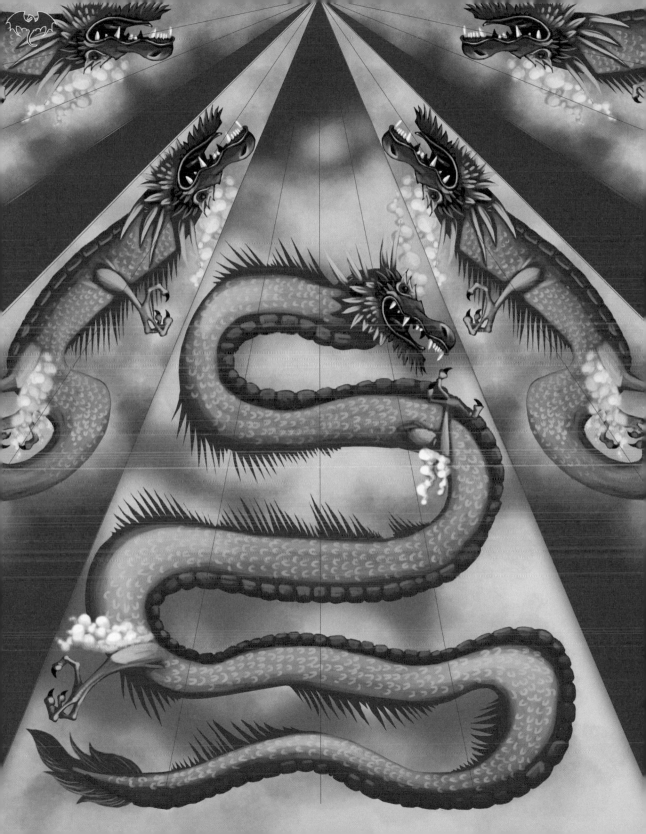

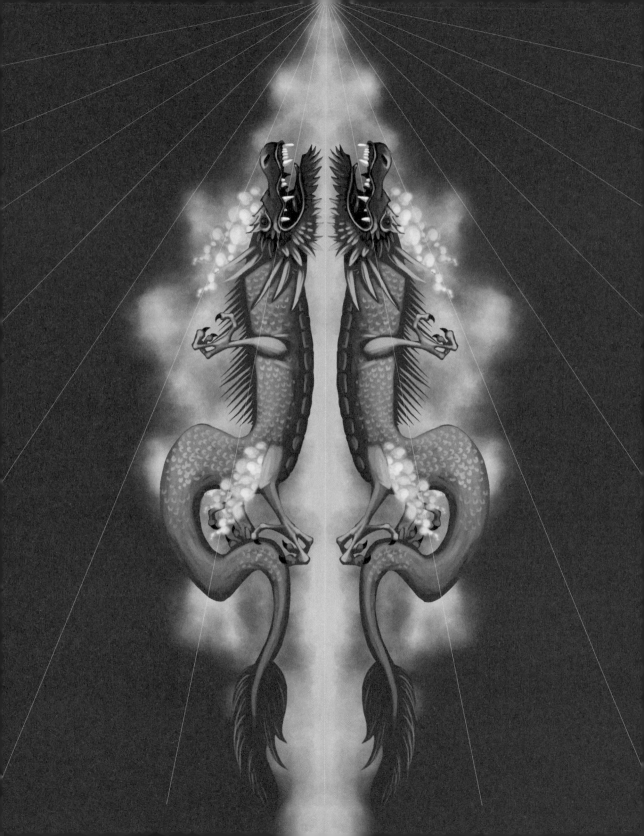

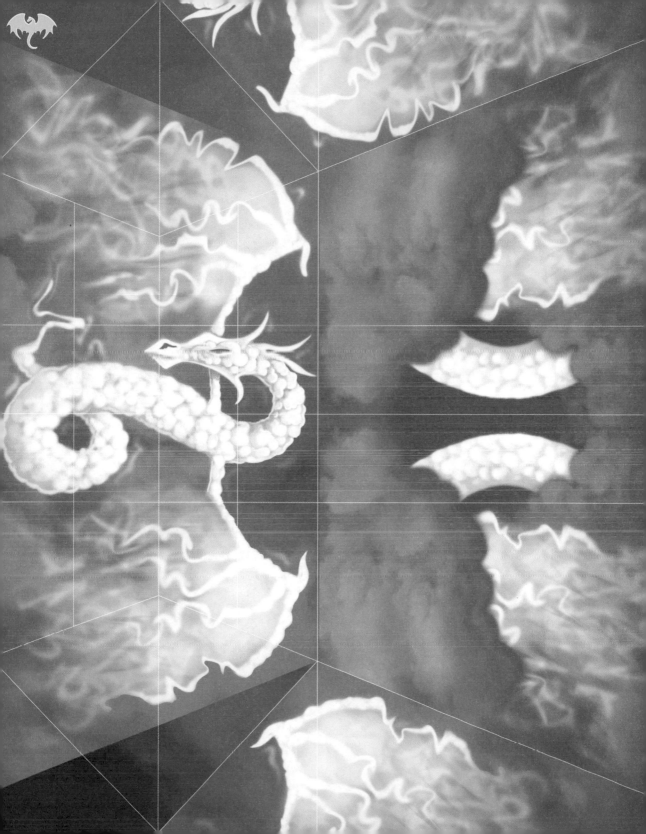

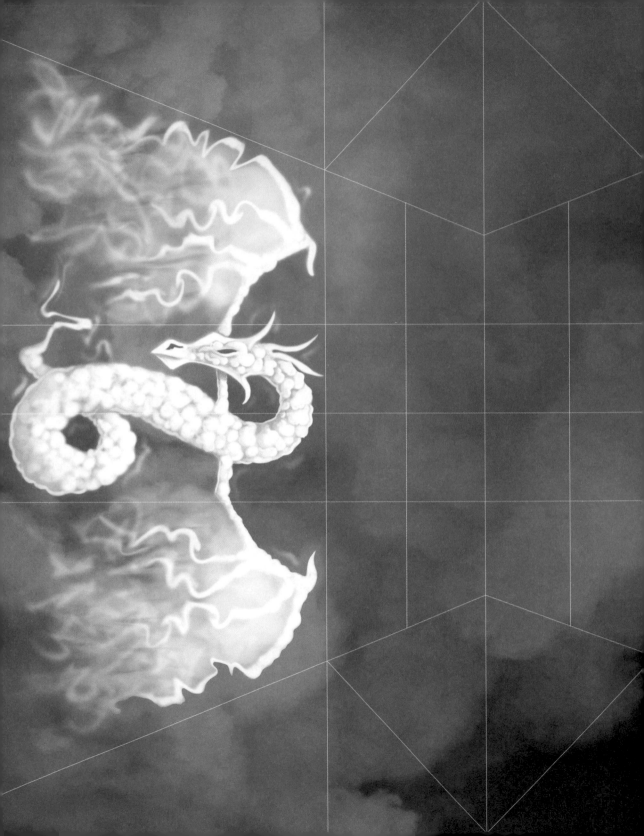

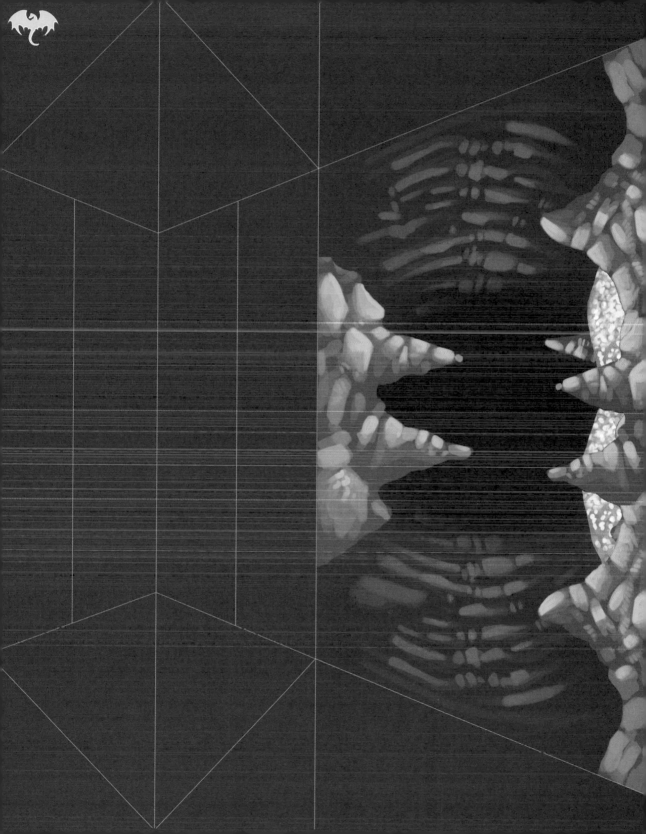

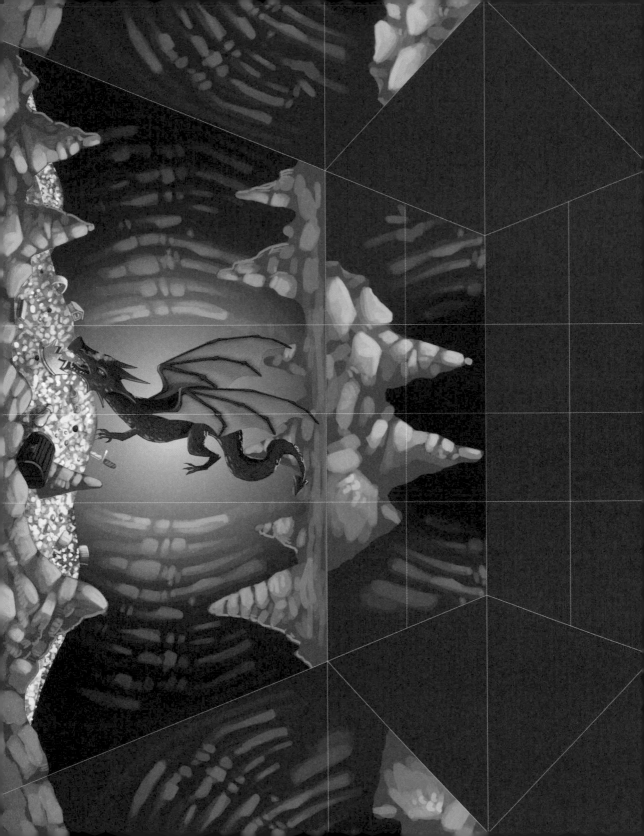

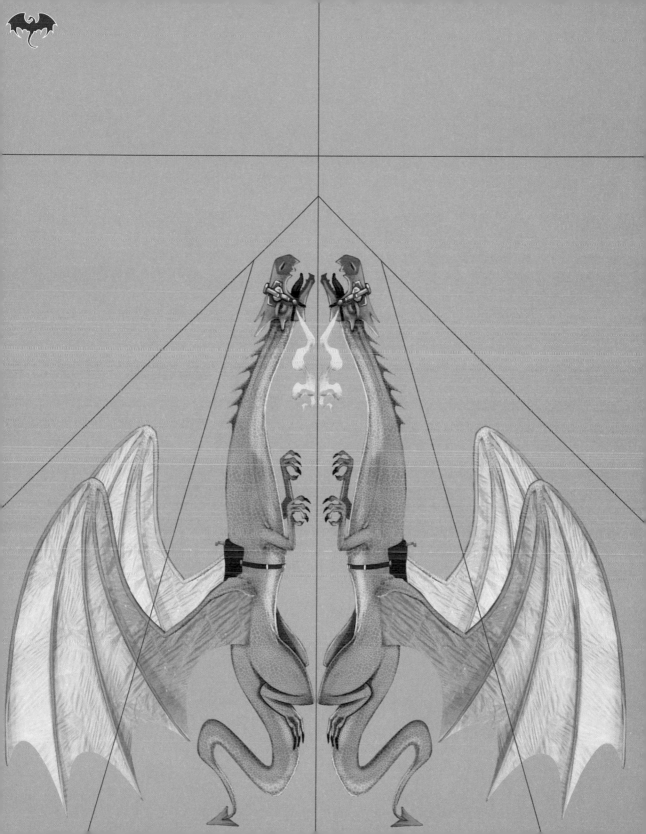

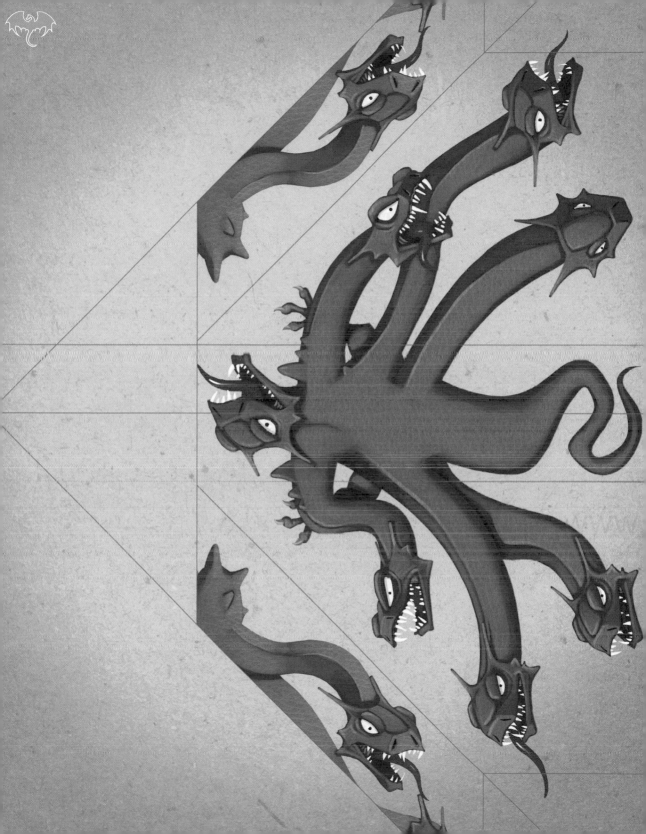

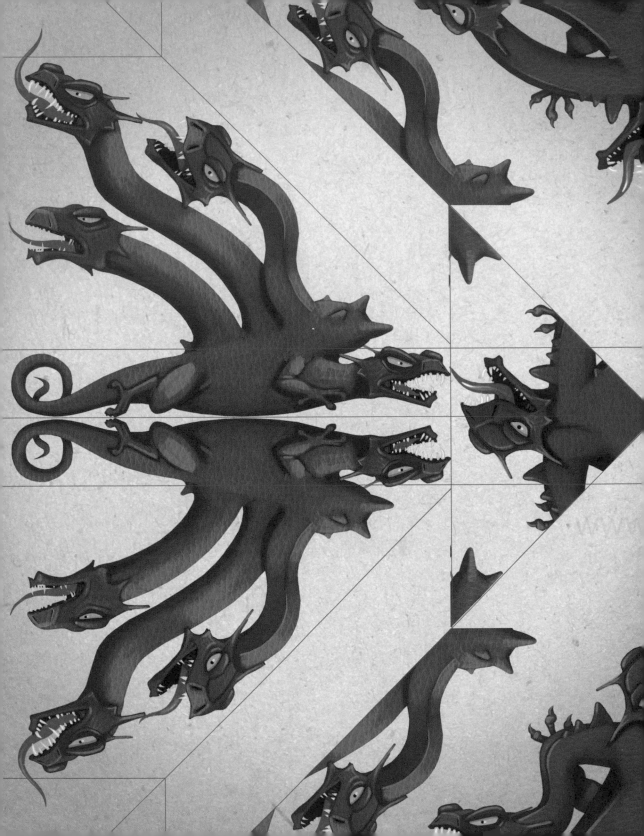

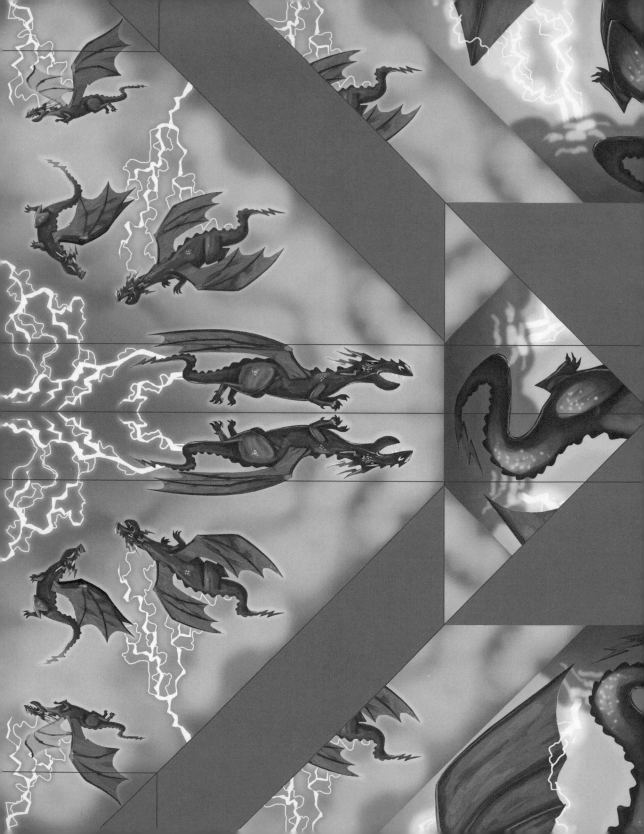

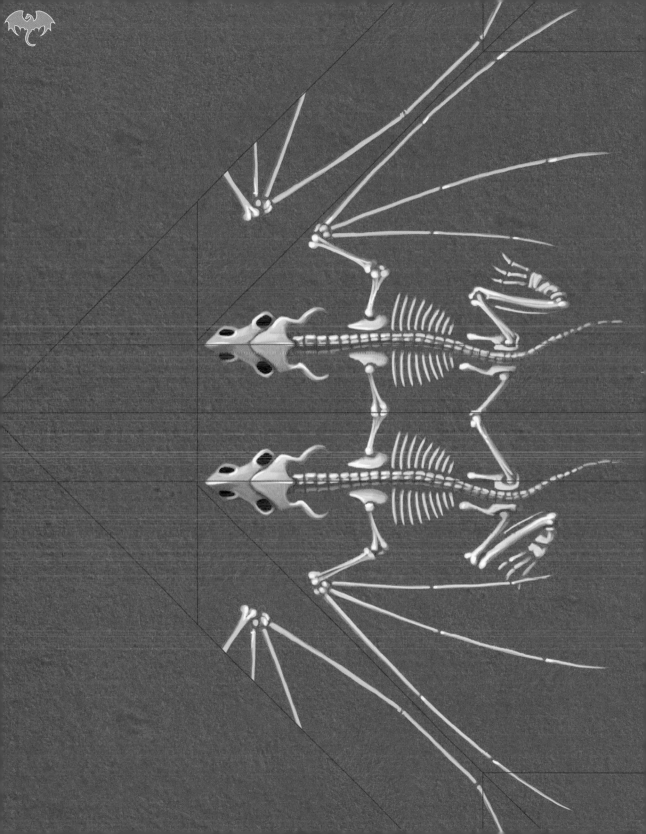

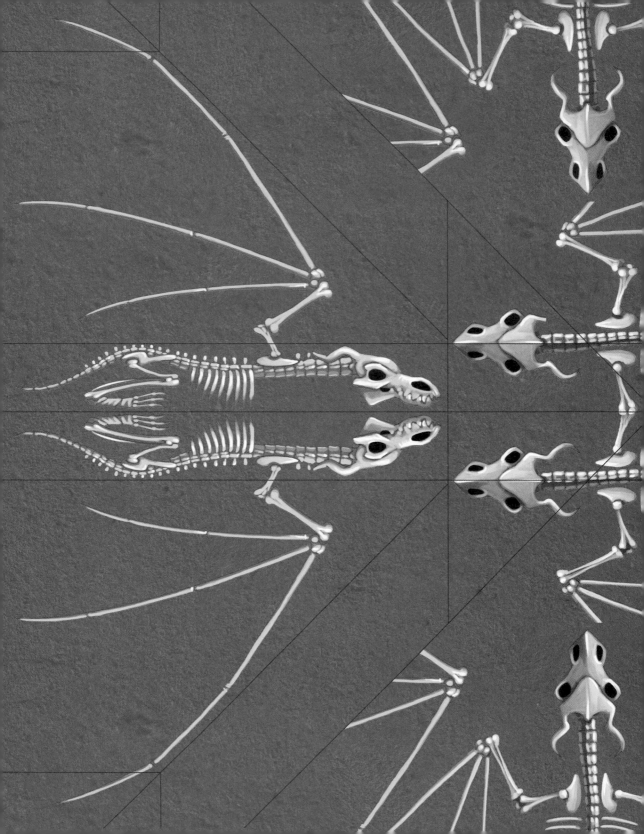

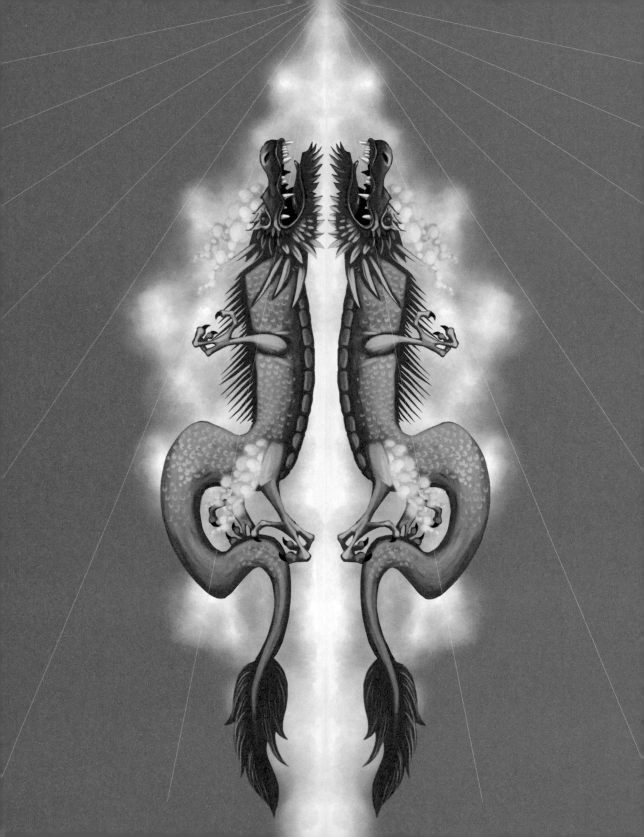

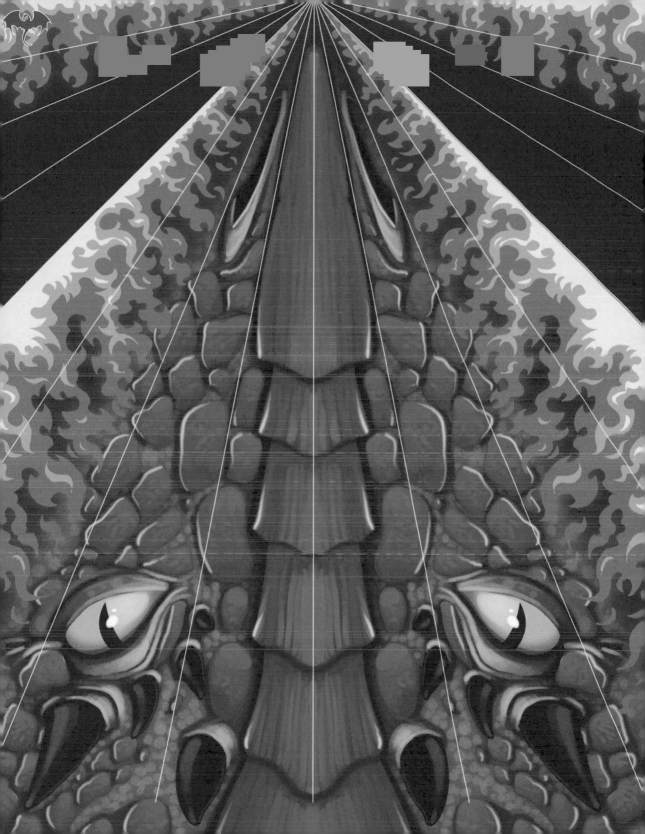

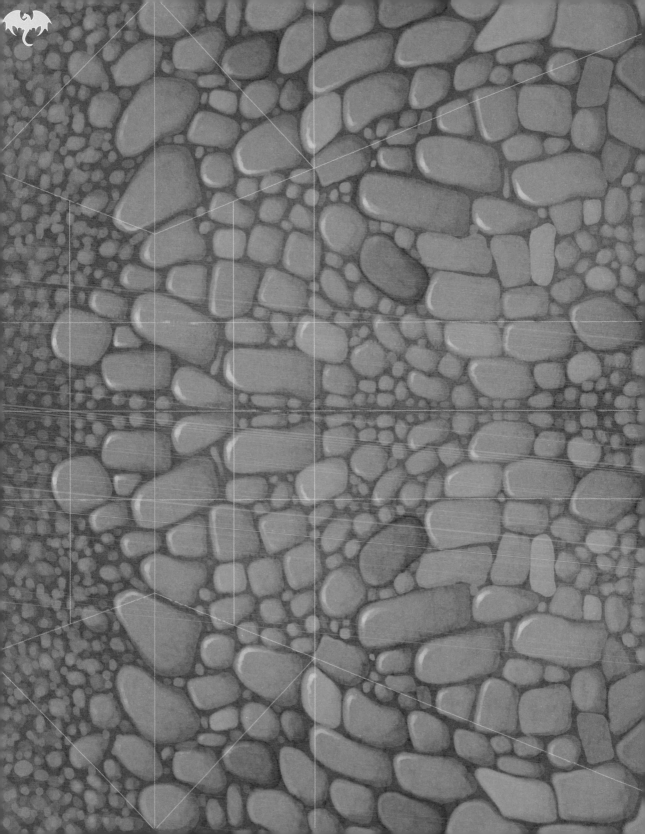

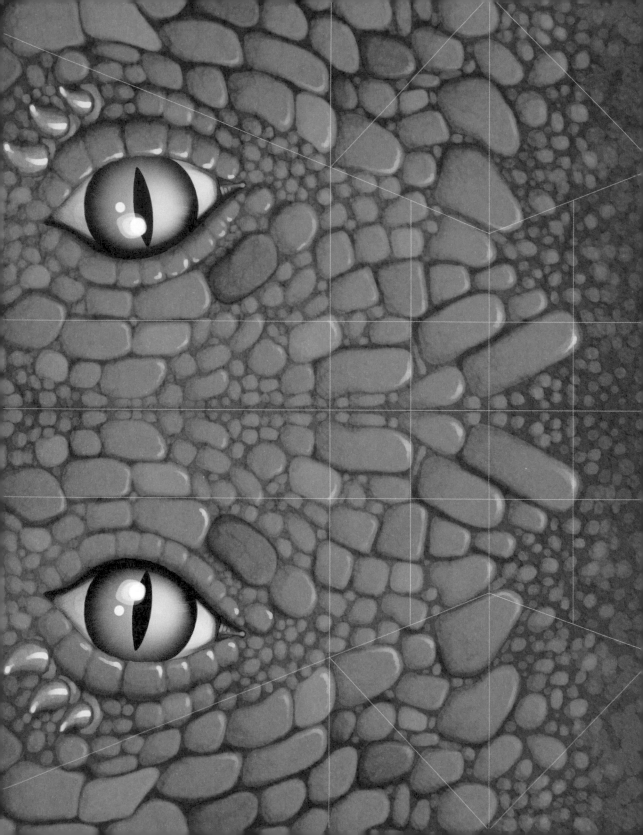

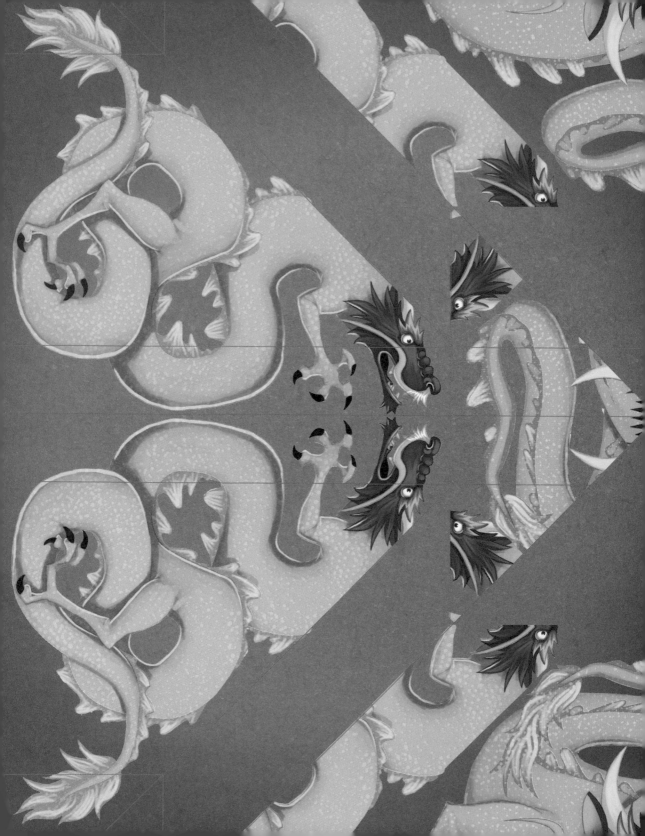

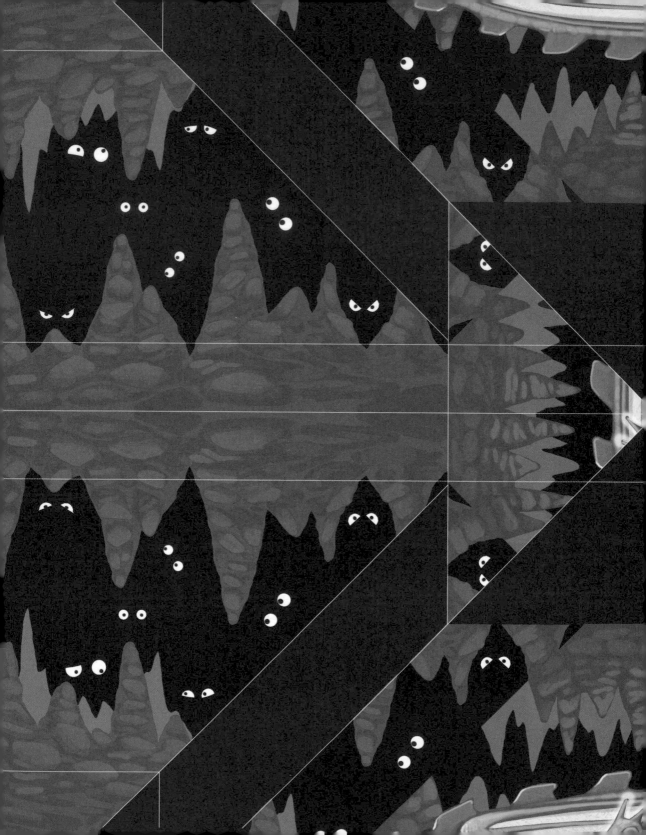

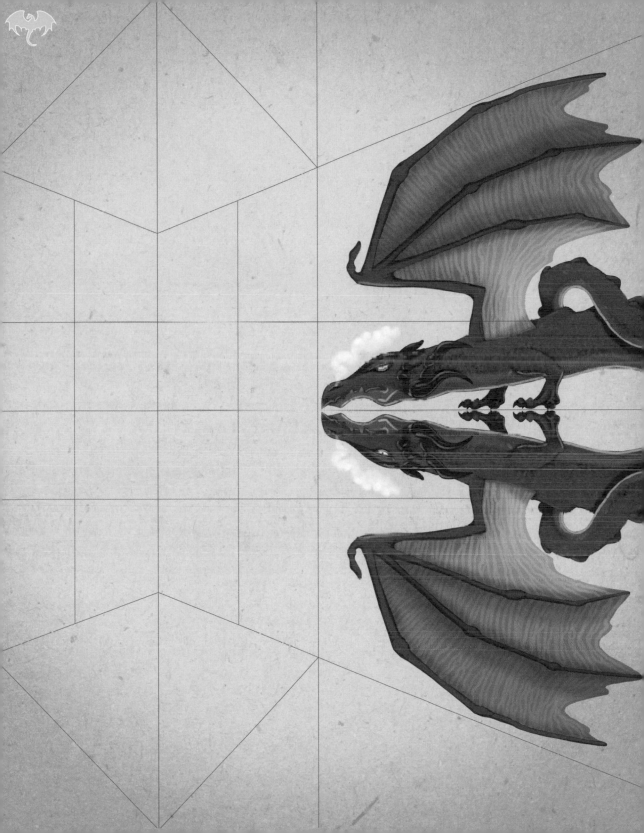

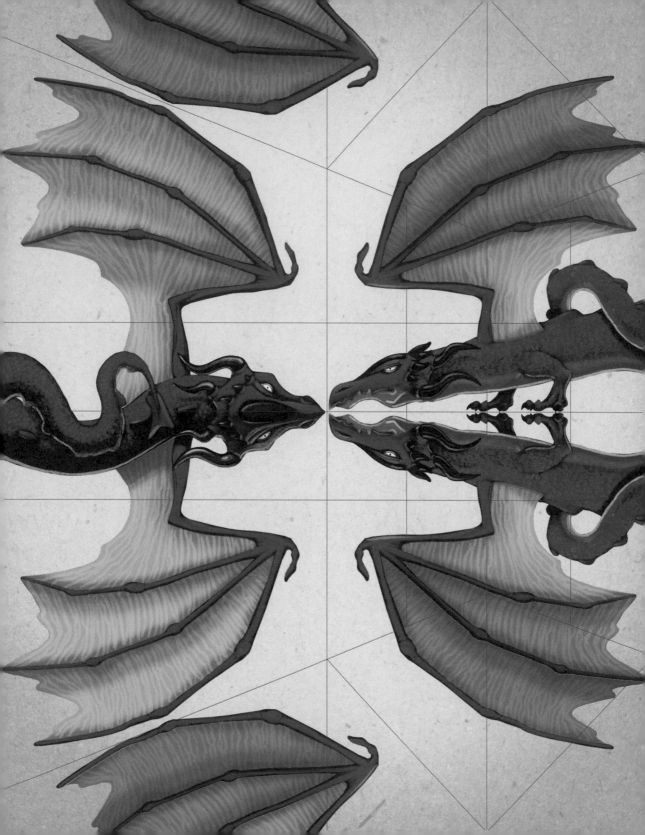

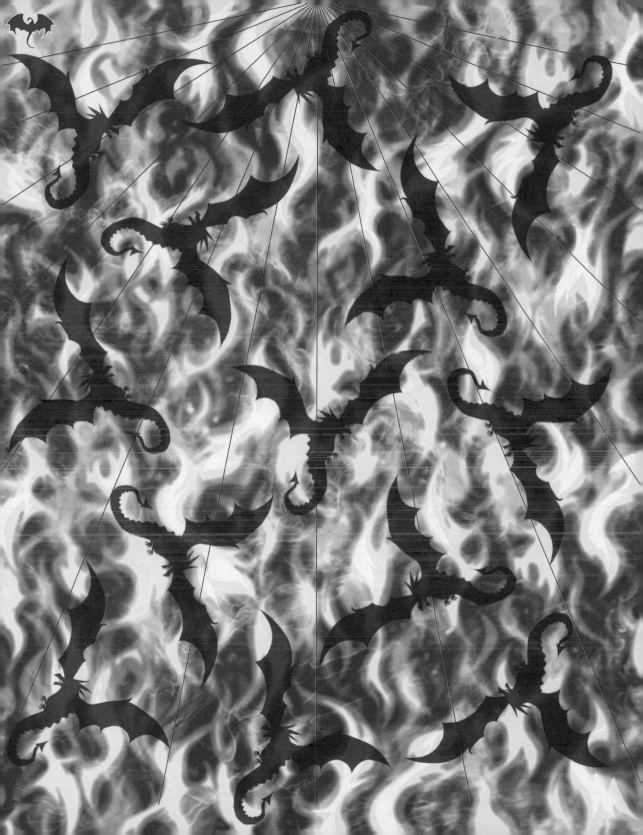

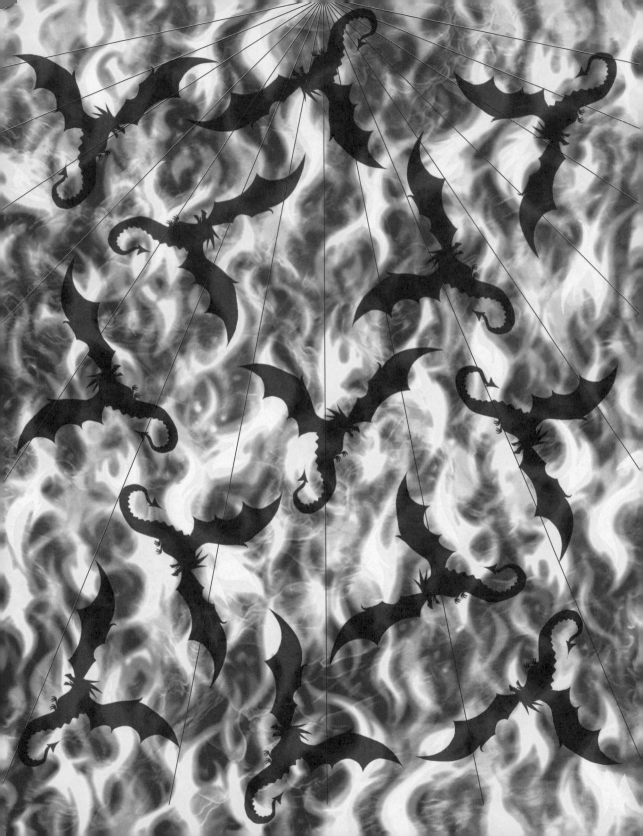

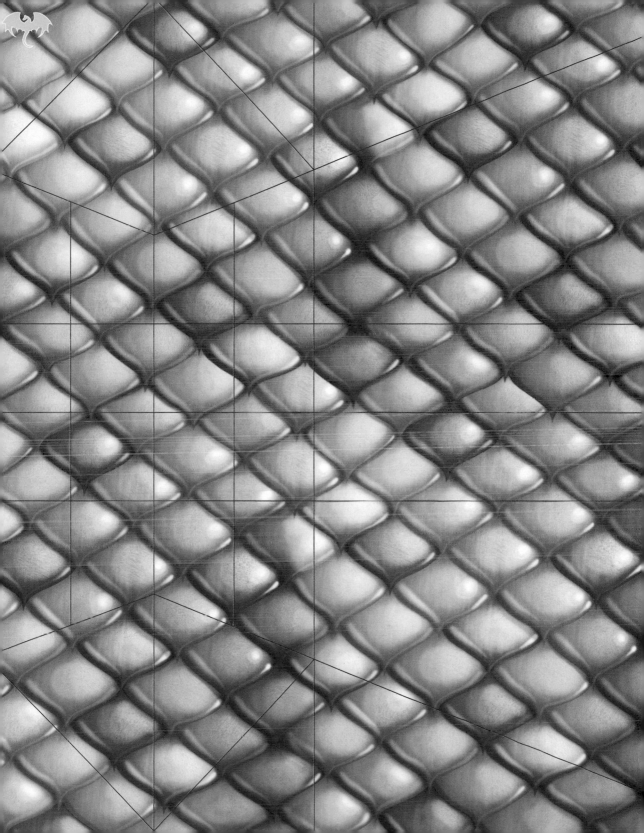

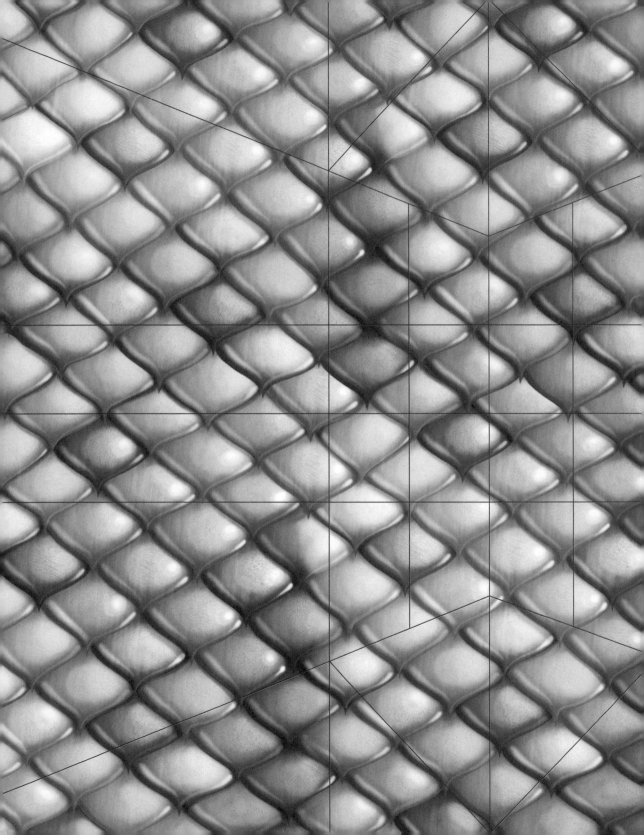

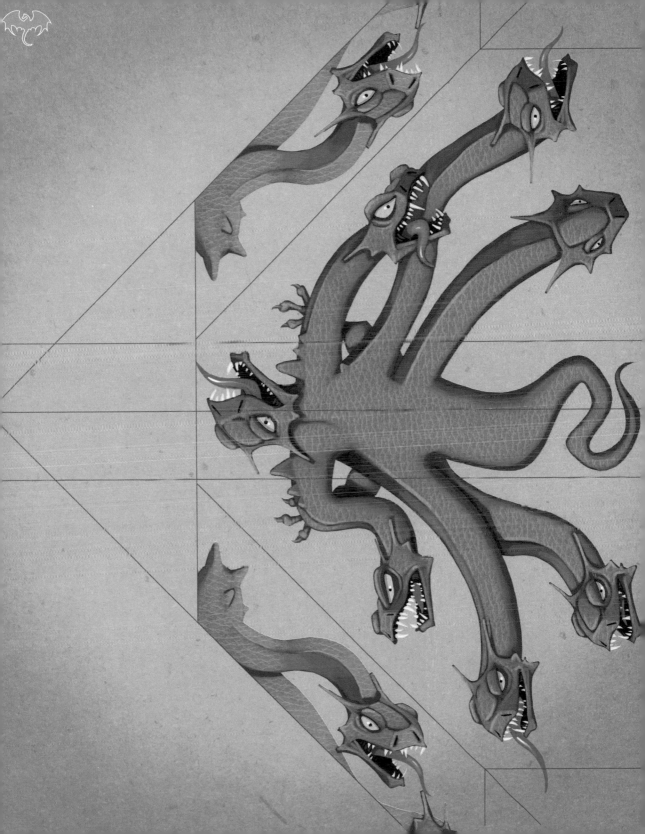